Rumpelstiltskin

First published in 2005 by
Franklin Watts
96 Leonard Street
London
EC2A 4XD

Franklin Watts Australia
Level 17/207 Kent Street
Sydney
NSW 2000

A CIP catalogue record for this book is available
from the British Library.

ISBN 0 7496 6153 4 (hbk)
ISBN 0 7496 6165 8 (pbk)

Series Editor: Jackie Hamley
Series Advisor: Dr Barrie Wade
Series Designer: Peter Scoulding

Printed in China

Rumpelstiltskin

Retold by Barrie Wade

Illustrated by Neil Chapman

W

FRANKLIN WATTS

LONDON•SYDNEY

Long ago, a foolish miller
told the King: "My daughter
can spin straw into gold."

The King locked the
miller's daughter into
a room full of straw.

"Spin this straw into gold by morning!" he ordered.

The girl wept. She didn't know how! Then a strange little man appeared.

"Give me your necklace, and I will spin all this into gold," he said. And he did!

The next night, the greedy
King locked the girl into a
bigger room full of straw.

Again, the girl wept.
And again, the little
man appeared.

"Give me your ring and
I will spin all this straw
into gold," he said.

And again, he did!

On the third night, the King locked the girl into a huge room full of straw.

"Spin all of this into gold and I shall make you my Queen," he said.

Again the little man appeared. "I have nothing left to give," wept the girl.

"You can give me your first child," said the little man. The girl promised.

So the King married the miller's daughter. Soon they had a beautiful child.

Then the little man appeared. "You promised me your child," he said.

"No!" wept the Queen.
"A promise is a promise,"
said the little man.

"But if you can guess my name in three days, then you can keep your child."

The Queen sent
messengers to find all
the names in the world.

She tried many names,
but the little man said
"No!" to each one.

On the second day, the Queen tried even more names. But the little man said "No!" to all of them.

That night, a messenger
saw a strange little man
singing by a fire in
the woods.

"The Queen won't win
the guessing game,
for RUMPELSTILTSKIN
is my name!" he sang.

When the little man
appeared on the third day,
he was sure he had won.

Then the Queen said:

"Hello Rumpelstiltskin!"

The little man was very angry. He stamped his foot so hard that he went right through the floor – and was never seen again.

Leapfrog has been specially designed to fit the requirements of the National Literacy Strategy. It offers real books for beginning readers by top authors and illustrators.

There are 37 Leapfrog stories to choose from:

* hardback